Christine Somersall O'Driscoll

Dedicated to Jim, my beloved husband,
and to my loving mother,
cherished children, grandchildren,
great-grandchildren and friends.

Christine Somersall O'Driscoll

My mother, Edith Bindon, was born and raised in Bute Street in 1935. She did not know how good a singing voice she had until her head teacher Mr Cezconus told her that she was singing in the Christmas concert. Edie has been singing ever since.

Now Edie is well known in Butetown for her vocal farewells at funerals. She also sang in a production of *The Tempest* which was filmed in and around Butetown.

When Edie is complimented on her beautiful voice, she says, “It’s a gift God gave me!”

Table of Contents

Introduction

In November 2014, Sian Holley (on behalf of Mind Cymru), produced an exhibition of Outside Art at the Butetown History & Art Gallery in Bute Street, Cardiff. She named the exhibition *Beyond Words* and, as well as a collecting the diverse and creative works of new artists, Sian also exhibited workshops and people's stories.

Karen Armstrong, a member of the BHAC, interviewed Christine and spent many weeks mentoring and helping to put Christine's memories and random writings together for the exhibition.

The results were an amazing mixture of fact and fiction, enough to turn into a small but interesting book called *Looking Back This is Me.*

Sian and I did some final editing and the results prove that nothing is beyond words...

Blessing to All My Daughters, Sons, and Husband

Always together, never apart,
All of my children are there in my heart
I love my beautiful children; they mean the world to me
There's so much I want to do for them, only they can see.

I also love my husband
I love him just the same
I love it when people say his name
He is sweet and harmless; he means the world to me
There's so much about him only I can see.
The children love him too, they often tell me, and I really
Understand them because they mean the world to me.
He also says the same words back just how they mean to me.
We have fourteen beautiful grandchildren
They mean the world to us
I'm never apart from any of them; they're in my heart you see.
Also, my three great-grandchildren and one on the way

My heart is with them too.

I have five beautiful sisters; I love them all the same
I get the same feeling when someone speaks their names.
All my friends they're all so good to me I thank them for everything
That they have done for me.
You always have your mother's touch because of the beautiful name

So what I am saying is from my heart
I love you all the same we will never be apart

God bless.

I Had a Dream

"No, No," the person said. "This is not a joke."
"Come with me and you will see a shining star by a beautiful tree."
Everyone ran to see the fun
the beautiful things this person had done
this is beautiful for everyone, even the animals are having fun.
So many games that they can play, things to do day by day, the beautiful sound of this ground where this tree was found.
Also, the river running down
Oh, what a beautiful sound.
Snowflakes and glitter blowing around.
"Please can you tell us where we are?"
"It's for me to know, for you to see."
Everyone was so happy, it was so sweet.
Then the person spoke
"Come now it's time to eat, there's plenty for you all."
"Even the animals can come around you've been running around all day long."
The stars in the sky flashing around and angels came in, big crowds flapping their wings as they hit the ground.
Yes, oh what a lovely sound.

Crown Him as King

My husband is a star
He never goes too far
He's always with me most days and that's the way things are

We do have our own ways
When things get tough
Between the two of us
We know never to give up

If I had my own way I would crown him king
And that's the way my feelings are for him

So what I'm saying from my heart
I always love my husband and I hope we never part

I do believe the red roses
I also believe in pink
I love the white ones
They make me want to blink
Ha ha

Always together
Never apart

Feelings

I get a certain feeling when things don't come my way
I feel like I want something but I can't have my own way
I get overheated, I know it's not the way
Don't get over heated best thing is to pray
People pray their own way
I feel the same
I feel there's only one God
But just a different name
My thoughts are with everyone
In the world everyday
I love to see daylight
That's when I awake
I also have my music
I play it through the day and listen to the beautiful songs
That people love to sing
It makes me feel much better by doing my own thing

So if you understand me, you know in your own way
Don't get overheated
Things will come your way

Talking Animals

One day as I was walking
I heard some animals talking
I thought I was dreaming
Until I climbed a wall
When I got to the top I had a fall
Sorry to the animals for scaring you all
Slowly they walked towards me
I gave a big call. Am I dreaming?
Did I hear you talk?
Yes you did
Please do not be scared we won't harm you
I felt so much better
I stood by the wall joining playing games with them all
Then I said goodnight
God bless to them all
See you tomorrow by the wall

Yes I do believe in talking animals
Do you?

Animal Farm

Ho ho, everyone, hope all is fine
Well not at the moment we are all down the line
Can I help you? I'll take my time
Yes we would be grateful, you're very kind
The children were saying you're losing the farm
I think I can help
It will be fine
Yes I hope so, the children work hard
Yes I know, in school they are so smart
Next week we are doing so much
Raising money for the farm
Thank you with all our heart

Billy the Snowman

My name is Jimmy
People think I am silly
Because I have a snowman friend called Billy
He looks so funny when he bends his head
He pretends that he is going to bed
The children run past him calling his name
Jimmy would join in all their games
One day he had to leave
To a place called home
Jimmy and the children shouted out his name
Please Billy will you come back again
Poor Billy snowman melted away
In the midnight winter
Frosty snow may fall
I will build Billy big and tall

Sailing Home

There's a ship sailing out of the bay
It's taking Dad and Grandpa away
Mam starts crying with tears in her eyes
While we stand there waving goodbye
Saying Mam please don't cry
Then she lifted her head up so high
As we walked down Bute Street
With pain in our feet
And runny noses not nice to see
Could not wait to get home for tea
There's loving Nan sitting home watching TV
Watching Coronation Street
Her favourite movie
Loving Mama making dinner to eat
Whilst we all sit by the fire
Warming our feet
Then we go running upstairs
To play games and jump on the beds
And before you know it
We were all fast asleep in bed
There goes that sound
Ho-Ho-Ho
That's when we know Dad and Grampy were
   coming home
Walking Bute Street never alone
Could not wait till they got home
Carrying their suitcases in their hand
Also boxes in the other hand
They walk through the front door

That was the big surprise
That was the good time when we
had so much fun
And Grampy shared everything
with everyone
Mam, Nan and all of us
Seen all the chocolate in the box

Back in the Day

Back in the day
When I used to play
We had fun and laughter everyday
Playing football, climbing, and running away
Taking no notice of what our parents say
Wouldn't be long before I would have to say
"Sorry, Mum, for running away."
"Come on, Sabrina, you're in to stay.
You've got school in the morning and all the next days."
Got told off in school today, detention again
Worrying now about what Mam will say.
When I come home, "Up the stairs," Mum would shout
"Don't slam the doors, you are not allowed out."
"I am really sorry, Mam, for detention today."
"Come on, Sabrina, this happens every day,
make sure you are good and you can go out to play."
I came home earlier the next day
"Well done, Sabrina. You can go out to play."
Saturday came and it was the best day
Something for us all to do and to play
One would make the fire
Whilst one swept the stairs
One would clean the kitchen
And one would make the beds
Well done, girls. You've done all you can
Now you can go and have some fun

Please be good and don’t run away
Don't be naughty, just do as I say
Sunday school tomorrow, it’s the day that we pray
Thank God for my mother
Thank God for everything.

Edie's Birds

Mam rises everyday
To feed the birds and watch them play
Up in the sky where the birds are so high
Mama would watch them fly.
They'd all come around when Mam sat down
Throwing the bread to the ground
Flip flap flip goes their wings
How Mam liked to hear them sing.
Back up to the sky they would all fly.
Before you knew it
They had all been through it
Oh look they're all coming back down
Pecking at the ground
Picking up things they had found on the ground
Like worms and bread
And things for their beds so the babies could lay their head
With a blessing through the night
Didn't hear a sound until daylight.
The beautiful sound of them singing
That's when Mama knew it was time for feeding.
There goes Mama sitting back down
In the same place where the birds come around
All the different moves on the ground
From the beautiful birds on the ground.

R.I.P. Mam
Love Christine

Childhood Memories

I wish I could turn back the years, back to the time when I was growing up.

I spent my time with my mother, Dad, Nan, and five sisters. Dad did not spend much time with us as he was a seaman and working away. I spent my days with my sisters and friends. Mam was the best mother in the world, and so was my nan.

I was born at 29 West Close, Butetown Docks, Cardiff. I went to West Close Nursery, then moved to Clarence Road School, and completed my education in St Mary's the Fitzalan High School.

One of Mam's rules growing up was that we went to Sunday school at St Paul's, and we attended weekly. I had some great times during the Whitsun school holidays with all my friends. I spent a lot of time playing games on a concrete patch in West Close, which would get icy during the winter months.

We used to use it as an ice skating rink. We played lots of street games such as hopscotch, touch-racing, and hide-and-seek. We played at Tomas Hoskins' (the paper factory) where we had lots of fun. During our games we always ended up by the canal, which for us was a very scary place.

As I got older, I spent a lot of time in Tug Wilson's shop on James Street, where there was a game machine. I stayed there until dark, when I would hear my mother's voice calling me, and I would run through the park as fast as I could.

Once we were all home from a day of fun, my mam would put a small oil heater on the landing to warm the bedrooms before we went to bed.

My routine was always the same. Days were full of fun with my best memories.

When I got older, I got a bit out of line by visiting places that I was not meant to. I would tell my mam that I was going to the Empire swimming pool, but would end up over the dock, swimming at C.H. Bailey's.

We made dens and called them 'Little House on the Prairie'. It was over at the docks at a place we called 'The Burning'. Mitching – it was so much fun. We would spend our day at the paper factory, go to our den, and then onwards to Alfie Baths, where seamen would go and wash themselves after being away for long periods at sea.

Near the flats where I lived, there was a local youth club called Chalkie White's where I spent a lot of my time. Mam would take washing to the launderette and we would collect it after school. Then we would go to our nan's who lived up on the top of old Bute Street shops. I loved to visit her every day.

We would also get tree blocks for Mum's and Nan's fire, and the rest we would sell.

I had a really special friend with whom I could share anything. To this very day we have kept our secrets –THANK GOD!!!

I suffer with epilepsy, which meant if I went to school and had a fit I would be sent back home. This was upsetting as it was not my fault.

Our mum did everything for us and we were so grateful for what we had. We washed our socks at night and put them by the fire to dry. We would then go out and climb walls, swim in the Wharf and jump off the crane. As soon as we heard our mam calling our names we would run home. When we were late I would always say sorry.

Me and my beloved mother – rest in peace, Mam...

The Little Girl and the Spiteful Girl

Once upon a time there was a little girl and her mother who lived in a cottage near the town.

One day Mummy said, “Come on, it’s time for school!” and the little girl quickly got up and rushed to get dressed.

As she was leaving the house, she hurried to kiss Mummy, saying, “Bye, Mummy, see you later!”

She felt the softness of her mum’s skin and the beautiful smell of coconut butter running through her hair with a lovely shine, something she would always remember. She opened the door and ran out with a cheerful smile on her face.

There was a lovely girl with beautiful red hair and the same features and smell as her mother. As she arrived in school, she made her way to her classroom with fear from the looks of the children who stared at her. She quickly became very scared and shaken up, because the children were always laughing at her.

There was a group of four children sitting around a table who said, “Don’t be scared. We have the same problem. Those children are always picking on us too.”

“Thank you,” she said and sat next to the four nice girls.

The teacher said to all the children, “Right, children, we will be performing a school play next week.”

“Yes!” screamed the children, as they all got excited.

Teacher replied, “I am going to need two children to be the angels.”

Many children put their hands up and yelled, “Me! Me! Me!”

The teacher looked and pointed out two children. The little girl was one of them; she could not quite believe it.

The spiteful children shouted, “Hey, that’s not fair! I want to be an angel too!”

One of them walked towards her and said, “Why should you be an angel? You’ve got ugly red hair!”

She looked up and said with a big smile on her face, “This will be my lucky day, with God’s help.”

Within seconds the school bell went. Everybody grabbed their coats and stormed outside to play.

The little girl and her four friends were playing nicely on the grass and talking about how two of them had been chosen to be angels.

Suddenly, the little girl looked around and shouted out, “Oh no! Those spiteful children are coming towards us.”

There was a big roar of fury from one of the spiteful girls saying to the little girl, "You will never be an angel!" to which the little girl replied, "Why not?"

The spiteful girl said, "Watch tomorrow. I bet I get picked instead."

"Okay," said the four girls, putting their heads up high. "We'll see!"

And the girl walked away with nothing else to say.

Ring, ring, ring, went the school bell again as everyone lined up.

The teacher shouted, "Everyone make their way to the school hall!"

As they made their way to the school hall, the children buzzed with excitement. The teacher explained that everybody had been told about the school play. "So when you go home, make sure to tell your parents to sign this slip for you to perform in the play."

The children quickly grabbed their coats and made their way home, skipping with laughter and screaming out loud, "I'm going to be an angel!"

The little girl quickly rushed into the house and shouted, "Mummy, Mummy! I have a slip off the teacher, will you please sign it? I'm going to be an angel in the school play."

"Oh, that's wonderful," replied Mummy, and signed it immediately.

The naughty girl stormed into her house and slammed the door.

"Hey," said her mummy, "What's wrong, sweetheart?"

The spiteful girl sat there with tears in her eyes. Her mummy took a soft tissue and wiped her eyes with a smooth, gentle touch.

Then the girl lifted her head and answered, "Mummy, we've been given a slip to bring home. There will be a school play going on."

"Oh, great!" said Mummy. "That will be lovely."

The little girl replied, "But I wasn't picked for the angel."

"Oh, sweetheart," said Mummy. "Is that why you were crying?"

"Yes," said the girl sadly.

Mummy said, "But you are an angel. You are beautiful too!"

The girl crept into the bathroom and started messing around with her mummy's hair dyes.

"Are you alright up there, darling? You've been in there a long time."

But there was no reply! The little girl had gone to bed. Mummy left her to sleep till the next morning.

The little girl glowed with excitement as she got up the next morning, had breakfast, and kissed her mummy goodbye.

"Bye, then," said Mummy. "Have a nice day."

The teacher said, "Good morning, children" and everyone said, "Good morning, Miss Brooks." Then they turned to the spiteful girl and laughed, making her even more upset.

The teacher said, "What's all this laughing about?" and everybody went quiet.

Suddenly one of the girls got up and said, "This is why, Miss Brooks," and pulled the girl's hat off.

Everyone laughed, and the teacher said, "I don't think this joke is very funny."

Everybody in the classroom went quiet.

Within a few minutes, everyone made their way to the playground. The spiteful girl sat by the wall near the door whilst all the other children were having fun and laughing. The friends that were near her did not ask her to come and play. They simply looked at her and laughed, then turned away.

Then the little girl said, "Jump!" and walked over to the spiteful girl.

Sadly everyone stopped playing, knowing what was going to happen now.

The spiteful girl was really sad, then the little girl said, "Don't be sad, I'm here to ask if we can be friends."

The spiteful girl looked up, her lips quivering. "Do you really think that?"

“Of course,” said the little girl kindly. “I’m really sorry that I laughed at you, but I understand why you did this to your lovely hair.”

Just before she could answer back, all the children came running up towards the little girl and the spiteful girl, joined hands, and started singing, “Sticks and stones may break my bones but names will never hurt me.”

The teacher was very pleased to hear everyone so happy and getting along for once.

“There goes the bell. Everyone in the classroom please.” And so they did with joy.

Then the teacher started to explain to everyone about the school play when the little girl jumped up and said, “Me, Miss Brooks.”

“Yes?” said Miss Brooks.

“Can’t the spiteful girl be the angel in the play? It’s just that the reason she dyed her hair was because she wanted to be an angel so very badly.”

“Oh,” replied the teacher, “that’s so sweet of you. Okay, class, please listen to what the little girl has to say.”

So the little girl got up and said, “Hello, everyone. I am giving my part in the play to the spiteful girl.” She smiled with joy, knowing that’s what friends are for.

The spiteful girl jumped up with joyous laughter and hugged the little girl hard.

The teacher said, “Okay, children, I’ve decided that both the spiteful girl and the little girl will be angels together.”

From then on, the little girl and the spiteful girl became best friends and everyone got on well and were friends.

Please do always remember to be friendly and kind to everyone around you.

Never Go With Strangers

Long ago there was Mum, Dad, and two lovely children whose names were Ethan and Jessica. Most days they would play in the garden and have so much fun, and they loved to play together with the ball.

Ethan always had a handsome smile, really thick, brown hair, and loved to wear his brightly-coloured tracksuit. Jessica used to sit, combing her beautiful long hair. She truly liked to dress up, dancing around pretending to be a queen.

One day they noticed the gate was broken and ran in to tell their mum and dad. Dad made his way into the garden and fixed the gate, making sure the children were safe.

Daddy explained, “You must not go by the gate,” to the children.

“Okay, Dad!” they replied, and carried on playing.

Suddenly, it started to get very cold, so Ethan and Jessica decided to go indoors.

“Is everything okay?” said Mummy.

“Yes, thank you!” whispered the children.

They noticed that Mummy was making something in the kitchen.

“Oh! Yes please, that would be nice!”

Then they quickly ran into the bathroom and washed their hands, and made their way back into the kitchen.

Mummy passed them an apron each then showed them what to do. They were having so much fun. They wanted to get the cakes done before Daddy came back!

It was time for everything to go into the oven and before they knew it, it was time for everything to come back out!

The cakes looked so beautiful, with a lovely golden brown colour, and lots of icing on the top. It was not long before Daddy came home.

Mummy showed Daddy the beautiful cakes Ethan and Jessica had made. He was so delighted, and sat at the table with everybody and enjoyed them. The day was very long for everyone so they all made their way to bed.

The next day, after everybody got up, Ethan and Jessica made their way into the garden and decided to play with the ball once again. They were having so much fun. Ethan kicked the ball so high it went over the gate – but he did not mean it!

"Oh no!" he said. "I must get that ball back."

"But how?" replied Jessica.

"Well," Ethan said, "I will climb over the gate!"

“No, no, no!” Jessica screamed. “You must not go over the gate. Daddy already told us we're not allowed!”

“I know I'm being naughty, but I must get the ball.”

Quickly, he climbed on the gate and jumped over. He ran to pick up the ball and then threw it back over into the garden. Whilst trying to get over the gate he realised he could not lift himself up.

Suddenly, a man with a weird hat, long hair, and a stick in his hand walked towards Ethan and asked, “Hello, would you like to see some puppies?”

“Oh, yes!” Ethan responded excitedly, and he shouted, “Jessica, I've met a man and he's going to take me to see some puppies.”

“No, no, no!” replied Jessica, “You heard what Mummy and Daddy told us... not to go with strangers!”

Just as Ethan went to say no to the stranger, the man grabbed him by the hand!

Ethan started screaming, “Help! Help! Jessica!”

Jessica ran into the house, panicking.

“Mummy! Mummy!” she shouted. At the time, Mummy was ironing the clothes and turned round with fright!

"What wrong, sweetheart?!" said mum in a panic, but Jessica could hardly talk because she was so scared.

"Calm down," said Mummy, and she sat Jessica on her lap.

Jessica explained to Mummy what had happened. Mummy quickly phoned the police, and called Daddy to come home straight away!

When the police arrived, Jessica was sitting in the chair really frightened. Daddy walked through the door and hugged Mummy so tight, wondering what was going on.

The police explained everything. Daddy spoke to Jessica and told her she must tell the police everything she knew. She quickly spoke to the police and told them what happened.

"Okay!" said the policeman.

Then off they went, with their dogs, to search for Ethan. All the police started to look for a missing boy with brightly-coloured clothes.

So far no luck, and it was getting darker, but the police did not give up.

One of the dogs started to bark!

"Over here!" shouted the police officer. "I found a shoe!"

Quickly, everybody ran to see. Not far away was an old house with trees covering every window. The dogs started to bark once again, then all the policemen got together and surrounded the house. One of the officers heard a big bang.

All the police made their way into the house. Every room was full with all types of things, like Hi-Fis, washing machines, clothes, toys, birds in cages, cats, and dogs. Even the animals couldn't breathe because the windows were blocked.

They made their way upstairs, pushed a door, and there was Ethan sitting in the corner, crying his eyes away!

"It's okay!" said the police officer. "We're here to take you home!"

"Oh, thank you, thank you!" cried Ethan. He was really delighted he was found.

While the officers were taking the stranger away, the others took Ethan home. The stranger was taken to the police station.

Ethan was glad to be home, and cried to Mum and Dad, "I'll never go with strangers again!" He hugged his sister and said, "I should have listened to you."

NEVER GO WITH STRANGERS!

Mr. Jim Mouth Organ

A long time back in the 1960s, in a beautiful place called Ireland where so many people would spend their time going to church, school, and shopping. The children spent most of their time on the horses – even playing in the fields climbing trees.

One day an old man walked through the field, shouting, "Come on all you children, you have been riding those horses for weeks! Don't you think it's time they had a rest? They'll be tired by the time it's show day!"

So all the children put the horses behind the gates of the fields, giving them to Rusty. The children quickly ran to the man and said, "How are you? What is your name please?"

The man said, "My name is Mr. Jim, the music man!"

"But why?" shouted one of the children.

"Because I love my music!"

But this man was very special, everyone in Ireland knew him, but the children had never heard of him!

"Up with you all now, children, come along. How about gathering some wood for my campfire?"

"Oh! Yes." And they all got together carrying as much wood as they could, then followed Jim music man, and placed it on top of his old campfire. Just as he bent down to light the fire, a small box fell out of his pocket. One of the girls picked it up and said, "Mr. Jim, music man, you dropped this."

He said, "Now thank you with all my heart! My mouth organ means the world to me!" Everyone looked!

"Why would something like a mouth organ mean the world to you?" and he sat down and asked all the children to watch the fire and listen to the beautiful story about his mother when she played the mouth organ, then left it to him. Then he started to play a beautiful song. It was so beautiful that half of the children fell asleep!

When he stopped he said to the other children, "It is getting late now, so I will drop you all home. You have to show me where you all live!"

The children helped Mr. Jim Music to wake the others and put them in a lovely pickup truck with a lot of hay in the back and everyone was careful.

Near their home by the side of the house, their parents were standing waiting for their children, wondering why they were not riding the horses, when suddenly Mr. Jim Music pulled up in his truck, got out and helped the children in the back of the pickup. He spoke to one of the mums.

"What are you up to, Mr. Jim Music?" yelled the mums.

"We heard all the old stories, Mum!"

The mums laughed remembering the old times, and all the children ran to their mums shouting, "Thank you, thank you, Mr. Jim! Night, God bless!"

He waved and said, "Goodnight see you tomorrow at church."

Next day, Sunday, everybody made their way to church. Mr. Jim Music got up and played beautiful music on his mouth organ - it was amazing! Just as church was finishing the children ran up to him and said, "Thanks for yesterday. Can we come again?"

"Right now your parents want to talk to me!"

When everyone got together they said to Mr. Jim, "We will be having an open day for the horses. It would be nice to have some music. Would you like to take part?"

Mr. Jim Music said, "Thanks so very much. That's nice of you all! Then all the parents and children sat down to have tea, coffee, and cool drinks. What a lovely day for everyone.

Back to the campfire for Mr. Jim Music, playing his beautiful sound. Just then came all the children. There was a big surprise for them all! When they sat around the campfire, Mr. Jim Music told them he was playing for the open day for the horses, and would they like to join in.

"Wow!" cheered all the children

"That would be great! But none of us have a mouth organ! How are we going to play without one?"

"Oh!" he said. "Can you keep a secret?" and with a cheer they all put their hands up.

He said join hands and so they did then all chanted, "Always together and never part!"

Mr. Jim Music got up walked by a rock, and picked up a beautiful box that he had for years. He sat down and opened it very slowly and carefully. The children could only see the most beautiful mouth organs just like his, passed down from his brother, Sister, Auntie, and Uncle. Now you must take care of them and look after them, then he pulled one out and said, "I am giving you one each you must be sure not to lose it! You have one each. I keep mine safely in my pocket. Some keep theirs under their bed. Everyone has his or her own place!"

Time was getting near to the open day, so every day the children would go down by the campfire with Mr. Jim Music and practice. They were all doing so well and before you knew it everyone had the tune right. All ready for that big day, but they kept their secret. Mr. Jim Music praised the children all for their beautiful music. Their parents did not have a clue. They thought it was only Mr. Jim Music playing.

The day came when the horse show was on. Everyone was getting ready to see the show. The big boys and girls getting all the horses ready, people walking past saying, "Top of the morning to you sir or madam" , and someone would reply "The rest of the day to you sir or madam" . As everyone made their way into the hall there was Mr. Jim standing up with a big smile on his face. Everyone was asked to sit down while they talked about the beautiful horses. All of the horses got first prize and they were so happy. The mums stood up to say thank you for all the help with the horses. Everyone clapped and one mum stood up and introduced Mr. Jim Music Man.

"As most of you already know him, for those who don't, he will be playing some beautiful music for the horse show." Just as he was going to play his music he winked his eye to all the children and they all got up walking towards Mr. Jim Music. Everyone wondered what was going on. When the beautiful sound of music started to play the parents were shocked by their children.

They were amazing. Everyone clapped till they could not clap any more. Mr. Jim Music Man called them all together and said, "You're all wonderful."

Mr. Jim was so proud of them all. "Well done, you all have earned those mouth organs. But you must carry on playing them."

"Yes," said the children.

"I am keeping mine forever."

"Me too," said the little girl.

The little boy said, “When I get older I am going to play mine to my children so they can go to sleep.” Another one said, “Mr. Jim Music, I am going to play a beautiful song for you to feel special.”

“Thank you, that is so kind of you!”

“Goodnight, God bless. See you tomorrow with God’s help!” Everyone shouted.

As he left he felt so special. All the children went home and talked to Mum about how they loved taking part in the open day. Everyone was happy and the children kept going to practice with Mr. Jim to play that beautiful sound.

A Christmas Wish

A long time ago there was a boy who would play with his friends. His friends were very nice to him and he was a very happy boy who was grateful for what he had, even though there were things that he wanted but his mum could not afford them.

One day his mum shouted from the front door, "Mickey, come on now, it's time for supper!"

"Okay," Mickey replied, quickly saying goodbye to his friends as he made his way through the door. "Hello, Mam," he said.

Mam told Mickey it was coming up to Christmas and Uncle Stanley would be coming to stay. Mickey asked his mum if his dad would be coming home too.

"With God's help, son," she replied.

Mickey said he would love to have a bike and Mam said she would try to get him one, but that she only had a little bit of money.

One day, when Mickey was walking home from school, he stopped to pick a wild flower beside the road. As he looked up, he saw a tall man walk past him. As Mickey got up to walk, he saw the man put his hand in his pocket and a piece of paper fell to the ground. Mickey picked the paper up and realised it was a five pound note.

"Hey there, Mister!" called Mickey.

The man turned around and said, “I can’t stop, I’m in a hurry.”

Mickey said, “Put your hand in your pocket and you will see you are missing something”.

The man checked his pocket and said, “Oh no! I’ve lost my five pound note! That was all the money I had!”

“I have it here,” said Mickey. “I tried to tell you, but you wouldn’t listen.”

“Thank you! Thank you with all my heart,” said the man. “Do you know where 29 High Street is?”

Mickey replied, “Of course I do, that’s my home, that’s where I live.”

The man followed Mickey to his house and when they got there Mickey rushed in to get his mother.

“Mam, Mam, there’s a man at the door!”

His mother made her way to the door, a big smile appeared on her face when she saw the man and they gave each other a hug.

“So this is Mickey,” said Uncle Stanley. “He‘s grown so big since the last time I saw him and he’s very well-mannered. He’s just found my five pound note and gave it back to me.”

“Very good, son,” said his mam.

While Mam made a cup of tea and some dinner she spoke to Uncle Stanley and Mickey about Christmas and said with God’s help Dad would be

The Magic Friendly Tree

Long ago, in a village called Woodlands which was near the woods, children would play all day-long, having so much fun they did not want to go home!

One Saturday afternoon, a few of the children said, "Let's go and play in the woods."

As the children were playing, one of the boys was standing there staring at a tree. Standing next to him was a girl. She was staring too, and then spoke to the boy. "Everything is okay."

Just as he went to speak, the rest of the children called, "Come on, are you coming with us?"

"Yes," they replied, and quickly ran over to everyone. In the woods was a beautiful conker tree and beautiful acorns, and also fir trees. Everyone would rush to get their conkers, filling their pockets up and also filling old buckets that they found. Some would fill rubbish bags that were blowing around on the ground. Some children would throw things at the tree, while some would climb it and try hard to shake the tree so the conkers would fall to the ground.

As everyone was making their way home, the boy and girl once again looked towards the tree. They saw something very strange, then ran to catch up with all the children.

Everyone made their way home. Before going indoors, everyone waved and said goodnight and God bless. Their mams and dads were amazed with all the conkers they had collected.

Before they knew it, it was the next day All the children playing out with their conkers while one boy and girl sat there talking about the tree.

The boy spoke to the girl: “Did you see anything strange about the tree we saw yesterday?”

“Well,” replied the girl, “I was not really certain, but I’d love to go back and look at it once more.”

“Okay,” said the boy, “Then we will, but we must not tell anyone. No, we must stick together and make this secret, okay?”

“Alright by me,” said the little girl, lifting her hand up high.

Making their way back to the woods, the two of them were very nervous. Once again, the boy and girl would stare at the tree, when suddenly the tree spoke, “Hello,” and made them jump!

The girl and boy grabbed hands. With shocked faces, they were very brave and spoke back, “Hello...?”

With a deep voice, the tree said, “Don’t be scared. I won’t hurt you.”

The boy and girl let go of each other’s hand.

The tree spoke, “Would you like an apple?”

“Oh, yes please,” said the girl.

They were so beautiful and red.

"Thank you," said the boy, "But don't apples only grow in the summer?"

"Yes," said the tree. "But I am a special tree. I can grow apples when I want to."

"Ho!" said the boy, "That must be great!"

With that, he sat down to eat an apple.

Then the girl said, "Don't you get tired standing up all the time?"

"Well, I get very bored. I love to play games."

Then the boy said, "I know, we can play a game. Like, we try to take your apples and you catch us."

"Oh, that sounds good," said the tree.

Then the two children would stand by the tree and try to get the apples, and the tree would kindly throw apples at them after the game for them to take home.

They had so much fun, but it was late, so they said, "God bless," to the tree and, "Thank you for the apples," and made their way home. They fell fast asleep.

Day after day, the children would go to visit the apple tree. It would always give them apples. They still kept their secret and never told anyone about the tree.

One day, as they made their way to the woods to see the tree, they noticed it lying on the ground.

"Oh!" cried the children. "What happened?"

They comforted and rubbed the tree, but the tree would not talk to them.

"Oh, Tree, please don't leave us!"

Suddenly, the tree said, "Could you get me some water?"

The children quickly ran to a pool of water and got as much water as they could. Then quickly threw the water over the tree, and with a big jump the tree popped up.

The children were so happy to see the tree awake once again.

"Thank you, thank you!" said the tree.

"That's okay," said the children.

They were so happy to see the tree talking once again.

Days went by and the tree was getting older and older and was losing its touch of magic.

Then it spoke to the boy and girl and said, "It is time for me to rest. I will not be here much longer."

"Oh," said the children, "Please don't go. We'll miss you so much!"

The tree dropped his apples.

The boy and girl joined hands and the tears ran down their faces. The tree disappeared and was never seen again.

The children kept their secret and never told anyone about the magic apple tree.

Talking Animals

Back years ago there was so many animals like chickens, hens, dogs and cats, you would not think to count them. Animals to some people are one of the most beautiful things in the world.

Long ago there was a little boy. His name was Jordon, and he lived with his mam, dad, brother, and sister. Mam would spend a lot of her time at home, but his dad, his brother, and his sister would go out to work every day. Their names were Mr. & Mrs. Chat, Antony, and Noreen.

One Friday evening, after school, Jordon came in and hugged Mam. He then asked if he could go down by the green field with his friends.

"Okay," said Mam. "But have your tea first."

"Okay," he replied.

After having his tea he ran towards mam, kissed her and said, "Love you, Mam."

"See you soon, son," Mam replied.

The green field was where all the children would go to play. They would have so much fun playing on their skateboards, swinging on the swings and climbing up the ropes – there were all kinds of things for them to do.

One day, Jordon decided to take a walk home through the back lane. As he was walking he heard a beautiful sound. He stopped and listened. Then he looked over a small wall and could hardly believe his eyes. He saw a load of beautiful animals all talking to one another!

He was so amazed he climbed over the wall, dropped down, and slipped right beside the animals. They all got very scared and ran into a big hole beside a tree.

Jordon was still lying on the floor like he was asleep, and all the animals slowly walked towards him and stared. The little cat ran to get some milk while the other animals held Jordon up.

Then the cat gave him a drop of milk.

Just then Jordon woke up saying, “I must be dreaming!”

The sheep said, “You had a fall.”

“Oh!” said Jordon, “Did you speak?”

“Yes,” said the sheep.

The chicken said, “We won’t harm you.”

“Oh!” said Jordon, “You are so sweet. Would you like to come and sit down?”

So the chicken did, and Jordon got very friendly. It did not take him long to get to know everyone, just like he got to know every one of his friends down at the green field, but he had just as much fun with the animals. He loved his new friends; they were so sweet, he did not want to leave them.

It was time for Jordon to make his way home, so he said to all the animals, “Bye! I will see you all tomorrow.”

He happily skipped home with a big smile on his face. Just as he ran through the door he shouted, “Hi, all!”

Dad said, “Jordon, have you noticed the time?”

“I am so sorry, Dad,” said Jordon.

Then everyone sat at the table. Dad talked about his work and Antony asked Jordon what he did that day.

“Oh! I had the best day ever.”

“Yes,” said Noreen, “Is that why you were late coming home?”

Mam laughed.

“Very funny,” she said, “He only went down by the green field with his friends."

Everyone was grateful for their food, said their prayers, and left the table.

Jordon was still sitting down saying his prayers.

“Are you okay?” said Noreen.

“Yes,” he replied.

He was praying for his friend.

“Upstairs,” said Dad. “School in the morning.”

Jordon gave Mam, Dad, Antony, and Noreen a kiss saying night, God bless.

He made his way to his bedroom.

After a long sleep, everyone got up and made their way downstairs for breakfast. Jordon was being very careful. He was going to school with his drink and sandwiches. Even though he had school dinners, he still liked to take something with him.

“All ready for school?” said Mam to Jordon.

“Yes, Mam.”

He hugged her, Dad, Antony, and Noreen and said, “Bye.”

Jordon was a very friendly boy.

At school, playing in the school yard, he hid by the side of a big bin. They were playing hide and seek, but Jordon made his way to see the animals.

He looked over the wall and said, “Hi, it’s me, Jordon.”

They all came running out of their hole by the tree and Jordon passed a bag to the dog. They all saw the sandwiches.

"Thank you,” they said.

“Okay,” he said, and he made his way back to school.

He was very lucky; the bell was just ready to go as he made his way right by the bin and pretended he was there all the time.

He made his way into the classroom sat down and listened to the teacher.

"Right," said the teacher. "Everyone will be taking homework home. It must be back within two days."

"Oh..." said all the children, even Jordon.

It was getting near home time, and one of children said, "Boys, are we meeting at the green fields?"

"Yes," said the boys.

But Jordon said, "I won't be coming tonight, I have somewhere to go."

"Oh," said the boys, "see you tomorrow then."

"Okay!" said Jordon.

As Jordon made his way home once again, he told Mam he had homework so he wouldn't be going to the green fields, he was going for a walk.

"Fine," said Mam, "but you must be home early. Dad would mind if you are late."

As he sat towards the table, putting bread and biscuits in his pocket, he also took all the waste food out to the bin. He was very good, but there was something up. Mam was getting very worried when he picked up the food bag.

As he got near the same wall, he came over and shouted, "It's me, Jordon!"

The animals ran towards him. They were so happy, they jumped all over him. He was so happy and sat down on the wall.

He gave the food to them all. He was taking Mam's food bag out to give to the animals. He should have told Mam, but he did not want anyone to know about the animals. He did not want to see them locked up in cage. He believed in setting them free.

They played so many games, and then they all sat down and talked.

"Well," said one of the animals, "tell us, please, what you did in school?"

Then Jordon did. He told them so much and told them he had homework. He must write a story

"That sounded very good. What will you write?"

"Well–"

As he stopped to think, the cat jumped up saying, "Why don't you write about animals? After all, we are your friends."

"Oh! Yes!" said the other animals, "It would be great!"

Jordon's face lit up with a big smile. They all danced, laughed, and jumped.

"Well," said Jordon. "It is time for me to go home."

"Hope your story goes well!"

"Thank you," said Jordon once again, walking through the line with a big smile.

When he got home, he got in before his dad, and he hugged his mam.

"I am going up stairs to do my homework."

"Good boy," said Mam. "I will call you when food is ready."

"Thanks, Mam."

As he went up to his bedroom, writing his story, Dad came home and he also hugged Mam

"Is Jordon home?" he asked.

"Yes," she said. "Is everything alright?"

"Yes."

Bro and Sister worked in the same place, so they came home together.

"Hi, Mum. Hi, Dad," said Sister. "How's Jordon? Is he upstairs?"

"What is he doing?" said Bro.

"Go upstairs and knock his door."

"It's only me, Bro."

"Okay, come in."

As he walked towards the bed and saw a book on it he picked it up and put it on the table, and then sat down.

Jordon sat on the bed and said, "Bro, do you believe in talking animals?"

He laughed, and then he said, "Yes, there is, but they have a way of talking."

"Like us?" said Jordon.

"Well..." said Bro.

"I have seen them."

"I've only seen a parrot talk."

Then there was a knock on the door.

"It's Sister."

"Come in," said Jordon, and she came in and sat down.

She asked, "Have you finished your homework, Jordon?"

Bro said, "He was just asking if I believed in talking animals. Do you believe in them?"

"Well," she replied, "I've never seen them, but it could be true."

Then Jordon read his story to them both. They were so pleased with him and they made their way downstairs.

When Mam came into the living room everyone started talking. Bro and Sister told Mam and Dad about Jordon's amazing story.

Dad said, "Please, would you like to get it, Jordon? Me and Mam would love to read it."

And so he did.

As Dad and Mam read it together, they were amazed and asked Jordon, "Do you believe in talking animals?"

"Well, yes," said Jordon, "Are there such things?"

Dad and Mam just looked without saying a word.

Everyone ate then made his or her way to bed.

Jordon got up the next day, ate his breakfast, and took the bin out, as usual. He hugged Mam and Dad and made his way to school. As he was on his way, he stopped once again by the animals. He stood on the wall and handed the food down to the dog.

"Thank you," said the animals. "See you later?"

"Yes."

Jordon ran to school.

Jordon was coming into school late and the teacher was worried why he didn't go to play over the green field anymore. One day the teacher wrote a letter to his mum and dad asking them to come to the school. She wanted to talk about the story and why he was sometimes late for school.

Well, just before the school holidays, Mr and Mrs Chat decided to go see Jordon's teacher at the school. The teacher was pleased to see them and she showed them into a room.

"I will get someone to keep an eye on my classroom."

Then the teacher made her way into the room with Mr and Mrs. Chat. They talked about the story he wrote, how amazing it was, and why he was coming in late for school.

"Also," said Mam, "I know he doesn't go to play down the green field."

"Oh, that," said Mr. Chat, just as the bell went for dinner.

Mr and Mrs. Chat were having a cup of tea. Jordon did not know they were in the school.

All the children decided to play hide and seek as it was their favorite game. It was Jordon's turn to go and play. As everyone was hiding, Jordon was seen by one of the children leaving the school. The child ran into the school shouting, "Teacher!"

Jordon got out of the school.

Mr. & Mrs. Chat heard the shouting and got up to see what was going on.

The headmaster asked, "What is going on?"

The boy said, "We were all playing hide and seek and Jordon went out of the school."

"Right," said Mr and Mrs. Chat, "We will find him."

Just as Mr and Mrs. Chat were walking out of the school, the Headmaster called, "Please, we will help. The children can get involved."

"Okay," replied Mr. Chat, and everyone got to walk through the line.

One of the children said, "Please stop, I heard something."

And so, everyone stopped to listen.

Then Mr. Chat jumped onto the wall and saw Jordon playing with the animals. He was scared. He thought Jordon was too, and got down with a strange look on his face.

Then the headmaster said, “Are you alright?”

But Mr. Chat could not speak, he was still shocked. Some of the children were too...

On the way to what was there.

When they saw Jordon playing and talking to the animals they could not believe their eyes. All they could do was laugh.

Mrs. Chat shouted, “Jordon, my love. It’s me, Mam!”

Then Jordon told the animals, “Be back soon.”

Then he said, “Yes Mam.”

Just as he climbed the wall he saw his dad, Mam, friends, and the headmaster. He was surprised to see everyone. Then everyone made their way back to the school and was told to go into the hall.

When Jordon was asked to stand up on the stage he was very scared, but Mam, Dad, and Teacher asked him so many times that all he could say was, “Please don’t take away my talking animals.”

So the teacher decided to say, “How about everyone get together and make the talking animals homes to live in and we can let them live in the school yard? They will be happy.”

“Oh, what a good idea,” said the children. “That would be great.”

Then Jordon said, "Well, I will talk to my animals."

Jordon went to talk to all the animals. When he talked to them they were happy they had Jordon as a first best friend.

Everyone helped to build homes for the animals. Then the animals were moved to the school where all the children played games.

And they lived happy ever after

Ha ha ha.

Do you believe in talking animals?

Jordon does.

Me too

Ha ha.

Publication Details

The stories contained within this book is a work of fiction. Names and characters are the product of the author's imagination and any resemblance to actual persons, living or dead, is entirely coincidental.

Typesetting & Printing by Octavo Publishing Ltd
Octavo House, West Bute Street, Cardiff, CF10 5LJ
www.octavopublishing.com